For Margaret McDonough McCarthy with love
—E. P.

And for my dear friend, Adelaide
—B. M.

The Mushroom Man

BY ETHEL POCHOCKI

Illustrated by Barry Moser

GREEN TIGER PRESS
Published by Simon & Schuster
New York · London · Toronto · Sydney · Tokyo · Singapore

GREEN TIGER PRESS
Simon & Schuster Building
Rockefeller Center
1230 Avenue of the Americas
New York, New York 10020
GREEN TIGER PRESS is an imprint of Simon & Schuster.
Designed by Barry Moser
Manufactured in the United States of America
10 9 8 7 6 5 4 3 2 1

Library of Congress Cataloging-in-Publication Data
Pochocki, Ethel. The mushroom man/by Ethel Pochocki;
illustrated by Barry Moser. p. cm. Summary:
A lonely worker in a mushroom factory finds
the friend he longs for when he meets a mole in the
park and takes him home to share his dinner.
[1. Moles (Animals)—Fiction. 2. Friendship—
Fiction.] I. Moser, Barry, ill. II. Title.
PZ7.P7495Mu 1993 [E]—dc 20 91-45106 CIP
ISBN: 0-671-75951-5

THE MUSHROOM MAN

THERE ONCE was a man who spent his days in the dark. He worked in a mushroom farm, a long, low, windowless building where mushrooms grew in beds of black soil and everything had the earthy smell of mold.

The man rarely saw the sun, except in the summer when it rose with him, or when it streaked scarlet-purple across the sky as he walked home after work.

When the people of the town saw him on the street, they snickered at his strange appearance. They called him the mushroom man, for indeed he did resemble the crop he tended. His round, oversized head was a bit too large for the rest of his body, and his flesh, pale as paste, was spongey to the touch. His deeply set eyes blinked often, and he walked slightly bent over, with soft shuffling steps.

Children would follow him, at a safe distance, and chant in their high singsong voices:

Watch out for the mushroom man,
The mushroom man, the mushroom man,
He'll eat you up in a frying pan,
Fast as he can, fast as he can!

Then their parents would call to them and tell them to stop that right now and come home, and they would run off laughing.

The mushroom man never answered them. He just kept on walking as if he did not hear. He knew he could not change their minds. They had already judged him by his appearance. They seemed to fear that they, too, might turn into mushroom people if they got too close to him.

The mushroom man accepted this without resentment, for he had been blessed with a cheerful disposition.

For the most part, he was quite content. Still there was this little ache now and then, sometimes dull, as in old

bones on a rainy day, sometimes sharp as a wasp sting. Sometimes it came when he was most content, because he had no one with whom to share his good feelings.

He knew the ache was loneliness, and he learned to live with it, as one would with a grouchy relative. "After all," he said to himself, "nothing's perfect."

He was comfortable living in the little basement room of an apartment house. When he got home, he would open a can of vegetable soup and a box of crackers and eat his dinner in the big brown overstuffed chair that made him itch, and he would listen to the news on the radio or the ticking of his wind-up clock.

Sometimes when the weather allowed, he would make a sandwich, stick it into his pocket, and go down to the river bank in the park. There he would sit on a bench and eat his peanut butter and marshmallow fluff sandwich, watching the strolling people and playful squirrels.

He found comfort in the antics of the squirrels. They chattered in front of him without fear. He would sometimes

offer them bits of his sandwich, which they would politely decline.

As he watched them, an idea began to grow in his mind. Perhaps he might share his life with a pet. A pet would be his friend, one who would like him just as he was. He knew it would not be a squirrel—they were too nervous to listen to poetry—or a dog. He did not like dogs. He supposed there might be some good ones somewhere, but he had been chased by too many whose snarling teeth had nearly nabbed him. No, it would not be a dog.

Suddenly the squirrels scurried, as a cat walked up the path towards the mushroom man, a creamy white creature with a superior air. She ambled past, ignoring him, then stopped to nab a flea on her rump. After disposing of it, she sat in the middle of the path, cleaning her ears, as if it were her private dressing room.

The mushroom man could not take his eyes off her. What a delightful creature! What exquisite coloring!

The cat looked straight at him, walked over, jumped into his lap, and put her paws on his chest. He noticed that she

was slightly cross-eyed, but that only added to her charm.

He stroked her white fur and rubbed her ears.

"Do you have a home, pretty one?" he asked.

"No," she purred.

"Would you like to come with me? I have sardines in the can."

"Yes," she purred even louder and licked his nose.

And so they left the park together and returned to his apartment. That night, as he settled into bed, the cat hugging his feet, he thought, "Now I am a completely happy man!"

He named the cat Beatrice, and she became absolute mistress of his home. While he worked, he thought of little else but coming home and spending the evening with Beatrice, watching her enchanting tricks and listening to her vast collection of songs.

Beatrice enjoyed the attention, the adoration, the chicken livers, the satin pillow—but after a while, she grew weary of it. Oh, the man was kind in a dull sort of way, but she was beginning to tire of being locked up and treated like a

delicate toy. At heart, she was not one who could be satisfied with hearth and home.

"I was born to wander," she sighed plaintively as she sat before the mirror, pluming her tail like a peacock. She decided it would be best for both of them if she left before the mushroom man became too attached.

And so one starry night as they sat on the bench in the park and he began explaining to her the position of Venus in the autumn sky, she quietly disappeared into a clump of yew bushes.

The mushroom man searched, calling out to her, pleading for her return, but Beatrice never came back. He sat on the bench, sighing sadly. Perhaps it was his fate to be alone.

The earth beneath his feet began to move. Something was making a tunnel. Then more tunnels spread out, criss-crossing each other like sled tracks in the snow. The plowing stopped. A small black-furred animal with a long, narrow nose burst from a tunnel and appeared to be checking out his workmanship.

"Helloo—" said the mushroom man softly, so as not to

startle the creature. The animal dashed back into the hole, almost missing it in its panic.

"Please come back," cried the man, "I won't hurt you! We could enjoy the evening together. I just want to be friendly."

After a short silence, a muffled response came from the tunnel. "We can talk, but I'll stay down here, thank you."

"Oh, please come out," pleaded the mushroom man, "whoever you are! It's such a lovely night. Don't you love the moonlight? I much prefer it to the sun."

A furry head appeared, slowly, cautiously. "I'm a mole, and I'll stay right here, thank you. You have a kind voice, but I can't afford to go around trusting anyone. You could be waiting to trick me with a trap or poison."

"You can trust *me*," said the mushroom man. "I said I won't hurt you and I'm a man of my word. You can sit over there by that clump of iris. I couldn't reach you if I tried. Come, share the moonlight."

"Don't you know anything about moles?" asked the an-

imal in weary exasperation. "Moles are blind. We can't see the moonlight or iris or anything."

"Oh, I *am* sorry," said the mushroom man, embarrassed. "I didn't realize—please forgive me."

The mole emerged from the hole completely. "Nothing to forgive," he said a bit too cheerfully. "That's just the way things are, and we do quite well, thank you, without sight. No point in making a fuss."

"I admire your spunk and courage," said the mushroom man.

"Well," said the mole, his voice quivering slightly, "I can stand being in the dark, but it's being alone that's difficult. I lost most of my family in a flood—I escaped when I was thrown headfirst into a drainpipe. The others were caught in a trap and made into a muff."

"I'm so sorry," the mushroom man said again. "I—I am quite alone myself. As for the dark, I'm rather fond of it. I think there's much to be said for being in the dark. Would you believe that I even work in the dark all day?"

"No, go on!" said the mole, wiping away the few tears that had escaped when he spoke of his lost family.

The mushroom man told him about the farm and how he picked and packed the pearly beauties by the light of his headlamp.

"Do you like mushrooms?" he asked the mole.

"The mole laughed, lightly at first, and then with such gusto he began to roll around in a patch of wild peppermint.

"What's so funny?" asked the mushroom man.

"*Do I like mushrooms?* My friend, mushrooms are right up there with worms and grubs! I could show you mushrooms you wouldn't believe. Right *now*—what do you say, are you up for adventure?"

"Of course!" cried the mushroom man, almost dancing at the thought of a shared adventure.

Off they went lickety-split into the deep woods. Even though he was blind, the mole was swift and sure of the path. The mushroom man could barely keep up with him. They came to an oak tree on a small hill, and the mole began to sniff and dig into the side of it. In a few moments, he

came up with something dark and squishy in the shape of a flattened ear.

"Truffles!" exclaimed the mushroom man, "the rarest and most delicious of all mushrooms! I haven't had a truffle in ages. I shall cook it up with a bit of butter and a dash of wine. Will you do me the honor of sharing this delicacy?"

The mole did not answer. He remembered his unfortunate relatives made into a muff. Could he trust a human?

"It has been a long time since I have had a dinner guest," the mushroom man said softly. "We could tell riddles and write poems and you could tell me about life beneath the earth. Do you like apple crisp?"

The mole decided to risk all. "Of course I will come. How kind of you to invite me," he said, knowing he had sealed his fate, for better or worse. And off they went, without further talk.

After dinner, which each assured the other was the most scrumptious ever, they ate yogurt-covered raisins and toasted their feet by the artificial fire (the mole, never having seen a real fireplace, said the crackling sounded quite real

to him.) They talked of many things and found they were in agreement about most of them, and then they said goodnight, promising to meet the next evening for dinner.

And so they did, and for every evening thereafter, until the trees were bare of leaves. With the first frost, the mushroom man invited the mole to spend the winter with him, and the mole accepted. The mushroom man brought a basket of dirt from the mushroom farm and set it up in the cool pantry, so the mole could burrow himself a bed.

During the day, the mole tended to the house—washed the dishes, shook out the rugs, made lentil soup and banana fritters—because he was very smart and remembered where everything was.

When Christmas arrived, they trimmed a small fir tree with cranberries and dried apple rings, nibbling as they worked. The mole gave the mushroom man a pair of sunglasses with sparkly red rims, a vanilla bean, and a poem he wrote about moon shadows dancing on the snow, as he imagined them. (The mushroom man framed it the day after Christmas and hung it above the fireplace.)

The mushroom man gave the mole a tin of worms imported from France, two pairs of green wool slipper socks, (one pair for the front paws, one for the back) and a music box that played *You Are My Sunshine.*

Each declared his gifts exactly what he most wanted, but they agreed, as they sat before the fire sipping spiced cider, that the very best gift of all was having a friend.

THE MUSHROOM MAN

was set in Palatino, a typeface designed by Herman Zapf in 1950. The lettering and calligraphy are the work of Reassurance Wunder. The illustrations were executed in ink and transparent watercolor on paper made by hand at the Barcham Green Paper Mills in Maidstone, England. The book was printed by Horowitz/Rae on 100 lb. Sterling Litho Satin, manufactured by Westvaco.

The whole was designed by Barry.Moser.